One Dat, Two Dat, Are You A WHO DAT?

A story for all ages about dedication, commitment, acceptance, and "Finishing Strong"

Written by Cornell P. Landry   Illustrated by Sean Gautreaux

PELICAN PUBLISHING
NEW ORLEANS

First published by Black Pot Publishing, 2010
First Pelican edition, 2023

---

*The word "Pelican" and the depiction of a pelican are
trademarks of Arcadia Publishing Company Inc. and are
registered in the U.S. Patent and Trademark Office.*

ISBN 9781455627196

Designed by Sean Gautreaux

Printed in Korea
Published by Pelican Publishing
New Orleans, LA
www.pelicanpub.com

A very special thanks goes out to my muse for this book, Lauren "Fleurty Girl" LeBlanc Haydel. If it were not for her pushing me to do a book for The Who Dat Nation, this book would have never come to be. If you look throughout this book, you will find characters wearing t-shirts from her clothing line.
www.fleurtygirl.com

Most importantly to my children, Bailey, Corinne, and Cooper, and to all the fans in the Who Dat Nation.

Thanks to Sean Gautreaux for all the hard work and dedication in finishing this book in a very short period of time.

"I am a Fan. A Fan I am."

"So, if I am to believe what you have told, you say you're a fan of the Black and Gold."

"Yes, I am a Fan. A Fan I am."

"Well, One Dat, Two Dat, are you a WHO DAT?"

"Did you Who Dat in your home? Did you Who Dat in the Dome?"

"I did dat Who Dat
in my home.
I did dat Who Dat
in the Dome."

"I AM A FAN.
A FAN I AM!"

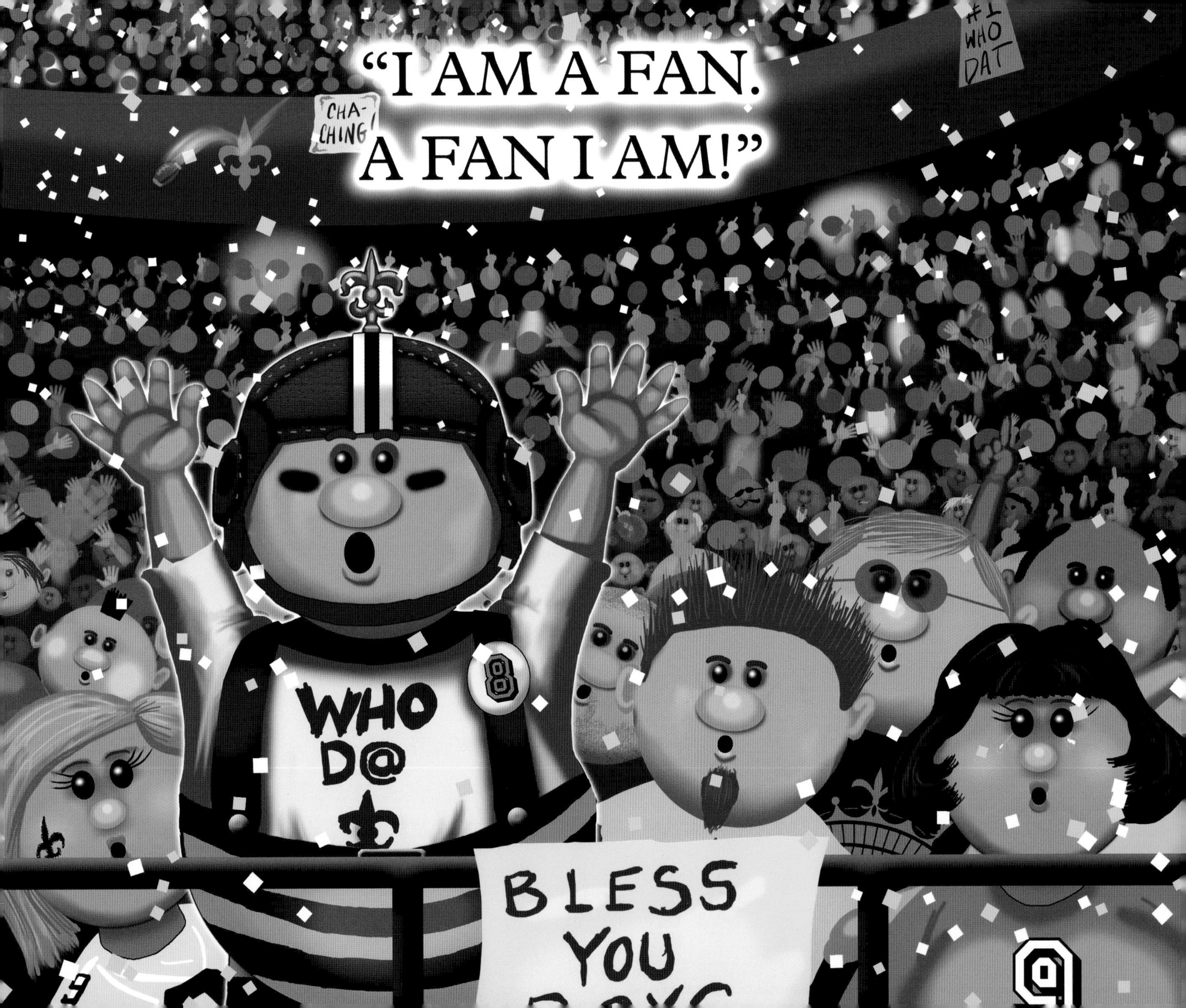

"Did you Who Dat in the Quarter? Did you Who Dat by dat Muddy Water?"

"I did dat Who Dat in the Quarter. I did dat by dat Muddy Water."

"Did you Who Dat in Jackson Square? Did you Who Dat everywhere?"

"I did dat Who Dat in Jackson Square. I did dat Who Dat everywhere."

"I AM A FAN!
A FAN I AM!"

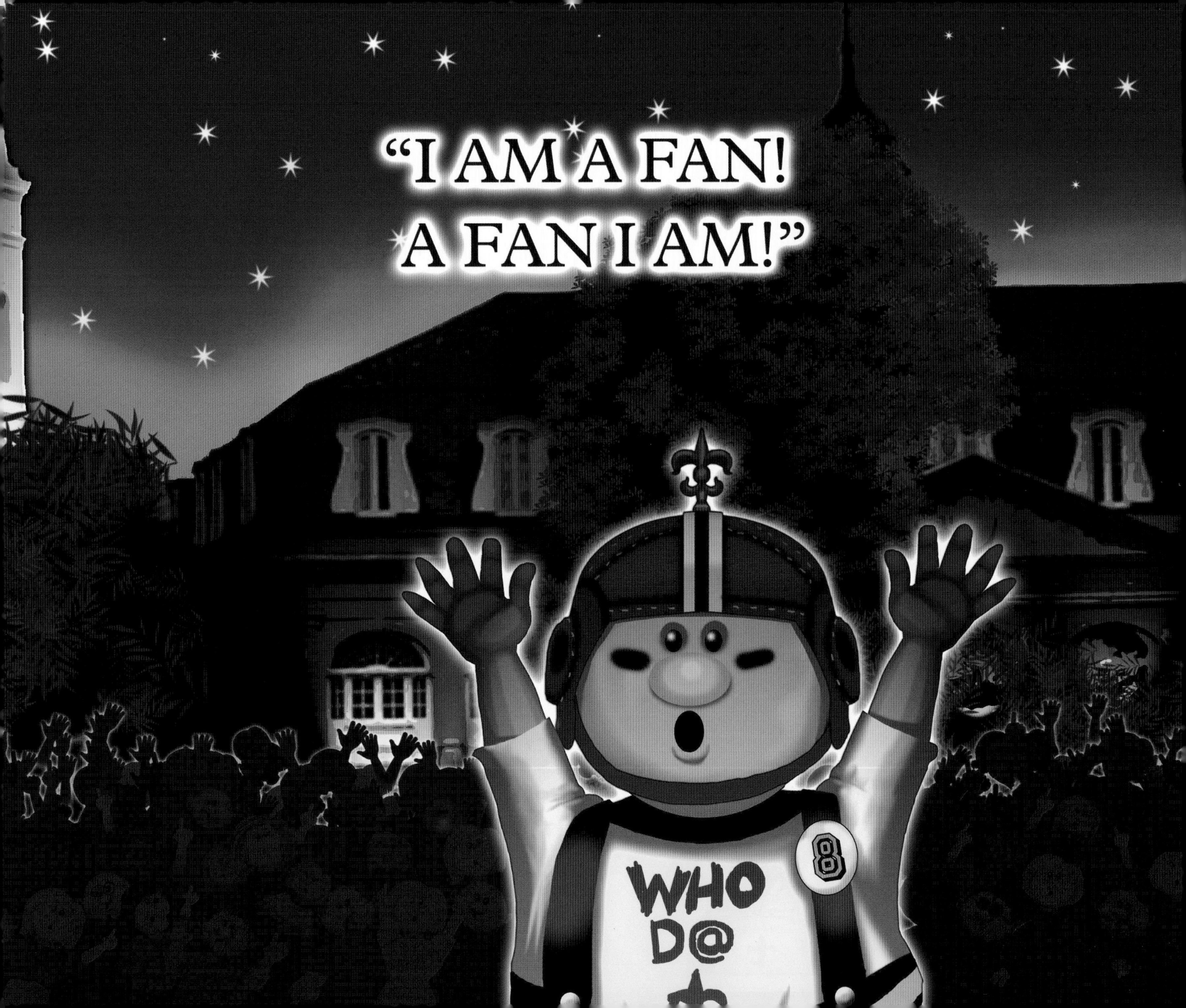

"Did you Who Dat with anticipation cheering those boys with jubilation? Did you enjoy dat great sensation all across this Who Dat Nation?"

"I did dat Who Dat with anticipation cheering those boys with jubilation. I enjoyed dat great sensation all across this Who Dat Nation."

"Did you travel
near and far?
Did you Who Dat
in your car?
Did you Who Dat
on a plane?
Did you Who Dat
on a train?"

"I did dat Who Dat
near and far.
I did dat Who Dat
in my car.
I did dat Who Dat
on a plane.
I did dat Who Dat
on a train."

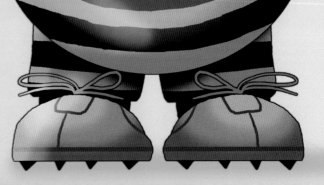

"I AM A FAN!
A FAN I AM!"

"Did you Who Dat in the Sun? Did you cheer and have some fun? Did you bring your entire family to the big game in Miami?"

"I did dat Who Dat
in the Sun.
I cheered those boys
and had some fun.
I did bring
my entire family
to that big game
in Miami."

"I AM A FAN!
A FAN I AM!"

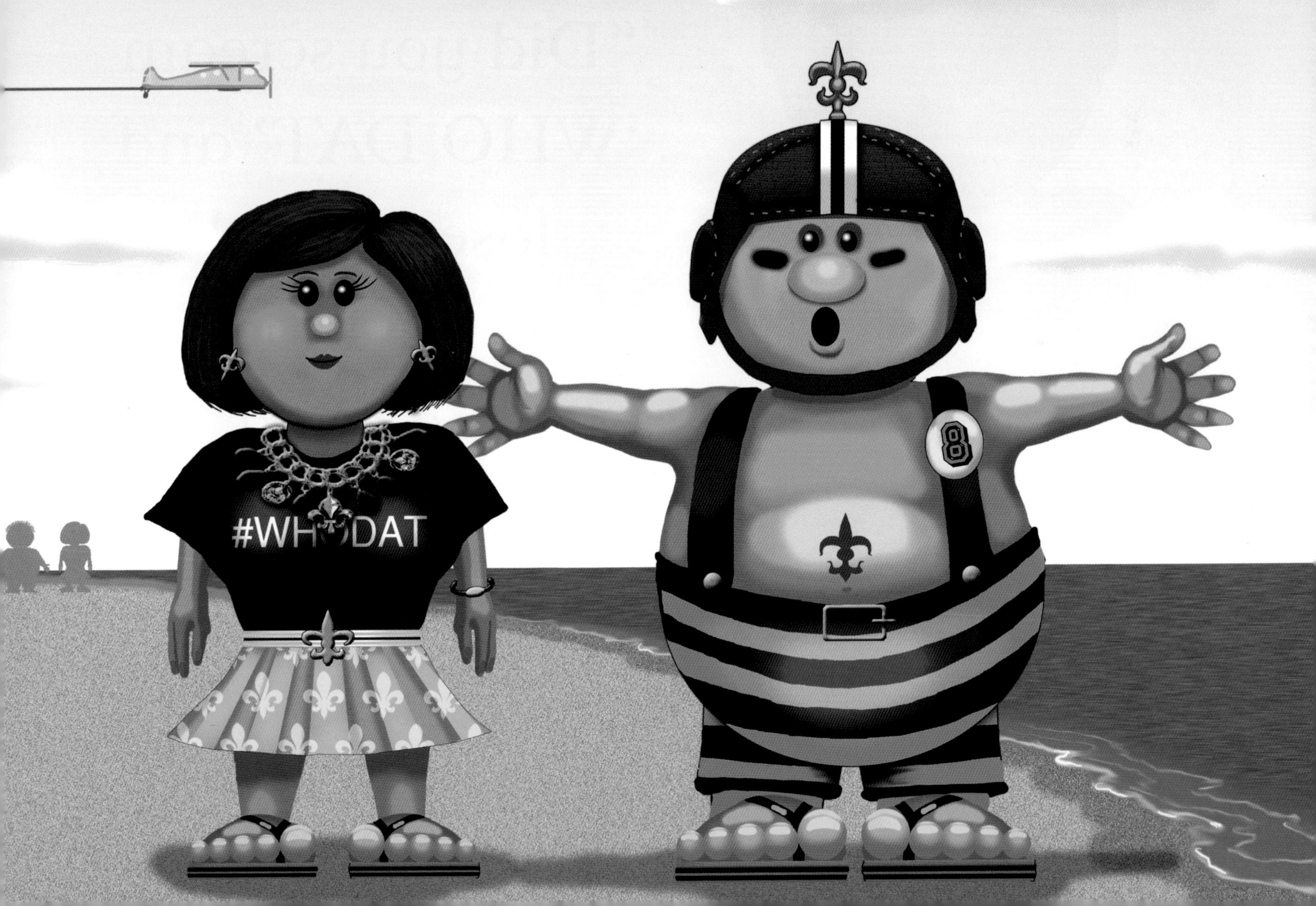

"Did you scream 'WHO DAT' and lose control as the Black and Gold won dat Superbowl?"

"I did scream 'WHO DAT' and lost control as the Black and Gold won dat Superbowl."

"I AM A FAN!
A FAN I AM!"

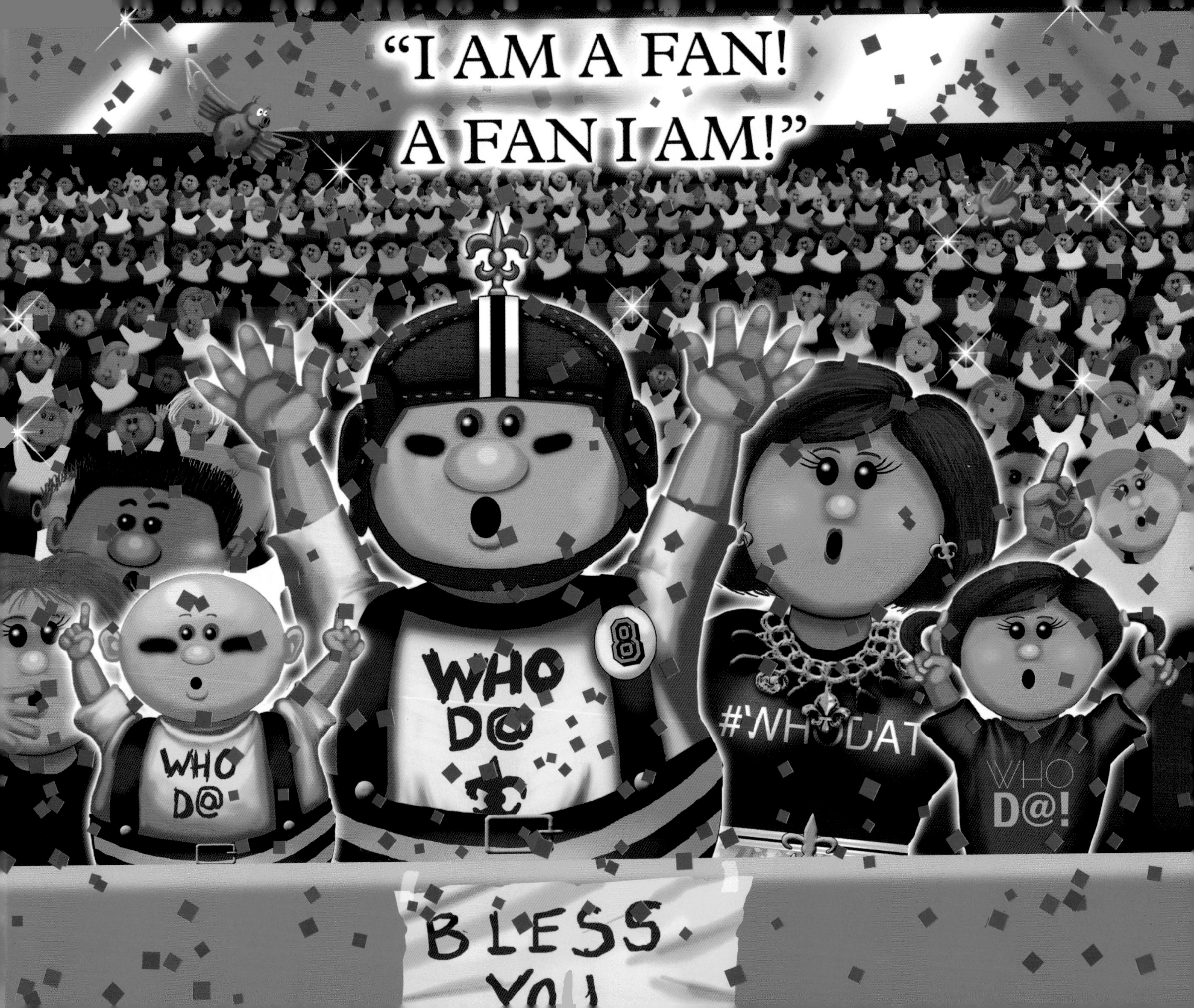

"You did dat with anticipation. You cheered those boys with jubilation. You enjoyed dat great sensation all across this Who Dat Nation."

"You did dat Who Dat near and far. You did dat Who Dat in your car. You did dat Who Dat on a plane. You did dat Who Dat on a train."

"You did dat Who Dat in the Sun. You cheered those boys and had some fun. You brought your entire family to the big game in Miami."

"You screamed 'Who Dat' and lost control as the Black and Gold won dat Superbowl."

"YOU ARE A FAN!
YOU ARE A FAN!
YOU ARE A FAN!
YOU 'FAN I AM'!
ONE DAT!
TWO DAT!

YOU ARE A WHO DAT!"

The Who Dat Dictionary

Alligator Pear: A Who Dat's Avocado

Ax: The way a Who Dat "asks" a question

Banquette: The cement path that a Who Dat walks on down the street. Most other places known as a sidewalk.

BoBo: (bow-bow), What a Who Dat calls a scraped knee, scratch, or sore.

Brake Tag: What a Who Dat has on the windshield of his car to show that it passed inspection. Inspection Sticker for Non Who Dats. *

Dis, Dat, Deeze, and Doze: The way a Who Dat pronounces "this, that, these, and those."

DoDo, Make DoDo:(dough-dough) What Mommy and Daddy Dats say when it's time to put da baby Dats to sleep. "Time to make dodo."

Dressed: The way a Who Dat orders his po-boy. Lettuce, tomato, pickles, and mynez (mayo for non-Who Dats)*

Hickey: What a Who Dat gets when dey bump dey heads.

K&B Purple: A certain shade of purple that only a true Who Dat would know. Named for an old New Orleans drug store.*

Neutral Ground: The grass or cement divider that separates two sides of a street. A median for non-Who Dats. *

Maw-Maw: What a Who Dat calls dey momma's momma/daddy's momma. A non-Who Dat grandmother.

Marraine (or Nanny): The female person picked at a Who Dat's Christening to be their godmother.

Paw-Paw: What a Who Dat calls dey momma's daddy/daddy's daddy. A non-Who Dat grandfather.

Parraine (Pah-Ran): The male person picked at a Who Dat's Christening to be their godfather.

Parish: It's a county for Who Dats. Louisiana is the only state in the union that has "parishes" instead of "counties." Who Dat!

Makin Groceries: What a Who Dat does when dey go shopping for food. *

Metry: A city just outside of New Orleans where a lot of Who Dats live. *

Pontchartrain (or Poncha-train): Da lake dat da North Shore Who Dats have to cross to get back home after a game. *

Shoot da Chute: What a Who Dat slides down at a park or a playground. A non-Who Dat slide. *

Where Y'at: A term used by Who Dats to greet their friends. If it's a male friend, usually "Where Y'at, Cap" (or "Podnah" or "Bra"). If it's a female, usually "Where Y'at, Hawt" (or "Daw'lin" or "Bay-Bee").

Ya'mamma'an'em: What a Who Dat says when they ask a fellow Who Dat how their family is. "How's ya' mamma 'an'em?"

Who Dat: A dyed through and through bleeder of the Black and Gold and what that means. If you have to ask, you're a non-Who Dat.

Gris-Gris: A little Voo Doo spell that a Who Dat uses on an opposing team to make them play poorly.

NEW ORLEANS: Pronounced either "Noo-Or-Lunz," "Noo-Aw-Lins," or "Noo-Or-Lee-Yunz," but NEVER "Noo Or-LEENS." Unless of course you are referring to the Avenue or the parish of Orleans. Or if you are singing about the city, as in, "Do you know what it means to miss New Or-leenz." If you are a non-Who Dat, you are confused. If you are a true Who Dat, you understand.

* Terms that you see with a * have shirts with the term themes on them available at www.fleurtygirl.net